THE DINOSAUR THAT POOPED EASTER!

Tom Fletcher and Dougie Poynter
Illustrated by Garry Parsons

PUFFIN

Danny and Dino's big Easter tradition
Was hunting for eggs on a chocolatey mission.

This year they were looking in Fairytale Land.
They needed some eggs for a feast they had planned!

They searched in the woods with their friend Little Red.
"We'll find eggs around Grandma's cottage!" she said.

But when they reached Gran's house, they all got a scare. They knocked on the door and . . .

They helped Little Red to rescue her gran.
Then Danny said, "Let's find more eggs if we can!"

So they set off to talk to the three little pigs . . .

They hunted up beanstalks . . .

and towers . . .

and more.

(While Dino munched all of the eggs that he saw.)

They found lots of eggs in a house made of sweets . . .
Then set off again to find even more treats!

Hansel and Gretel said,
"Time to be brave! Let's follow
this trail to a magical cave . . ."

"WOW!" shouted Danny. "We've found eggs galore!"
He picked up the biggest, but then heard a . . .

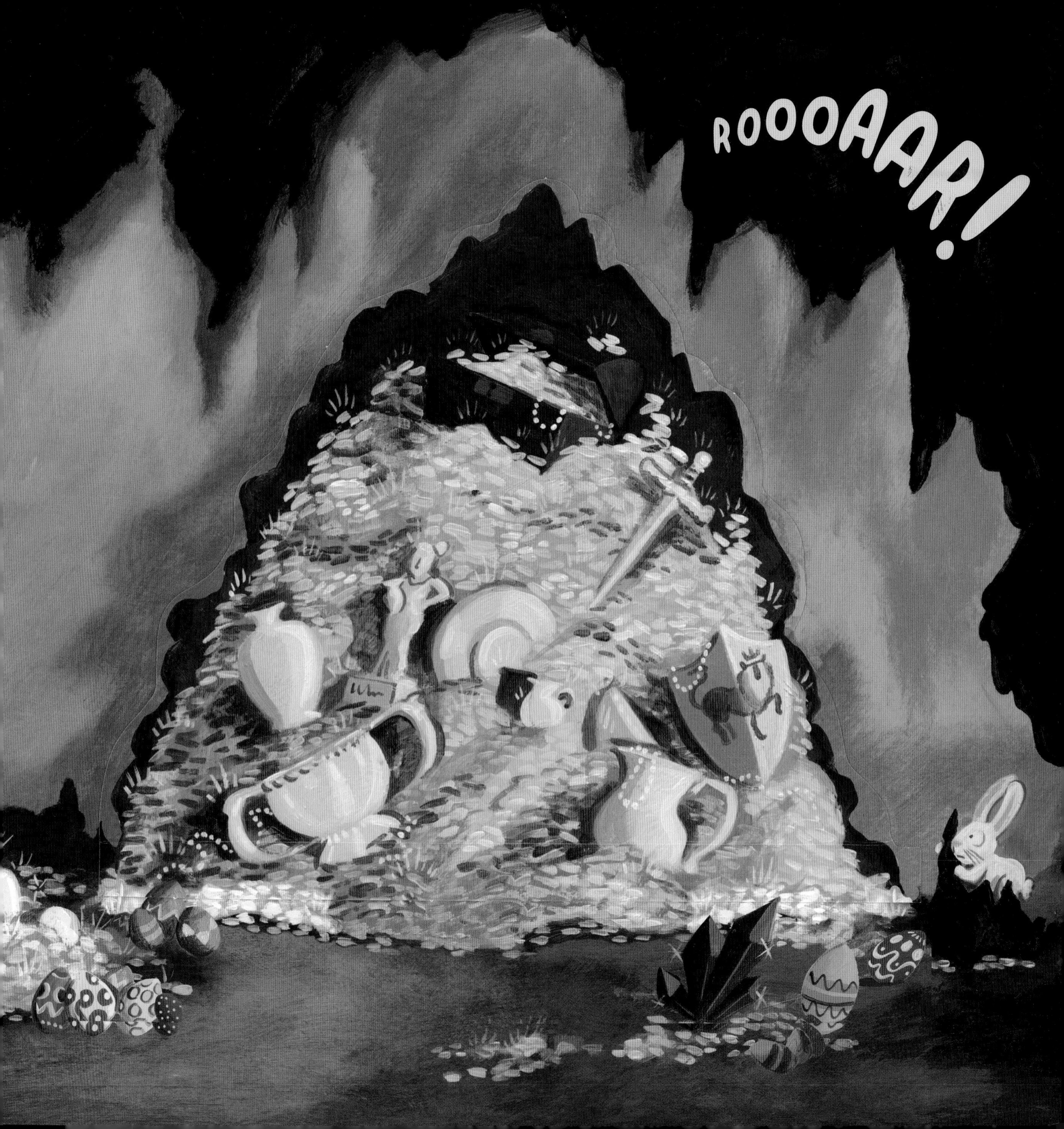
ROOOAAR!

With chocolate still swirling inside Dino's gut,
His brain brewed a plan involving his butt.

The dragon was coming, but Dinosaur knew
To escape from the cave he needed to . . .

They whooshed from the cave,
flinging muck far and wide,
As chocolate kept coming
from Dino's backside.

The big scaly dragon began to give chase
Till chocolatey poop splashed her right in the face.

The land was a mess and was starting to smell . . .

... made enough treats for the best Easter ever!

The feast was a hit! Everyone was delighted . . .

To Buzz, Buddy and Max – T.F.
To Reggie – D.P.
For Kyle and Codie – G.P.

PUFFIN BOOKS
UK | USA | Canada | Ireland | Australia
India | New Zealand | South Africa
Puffin Books is part of the Penguin Random House group of companies
whose addresses can be found at global.penguinrandomhouse.com.

First published 2023
001
Copyright © Tom Fletcher and Dougie Poynter, 2023
Illustrated by Garry Parsons
The moral right of the authors has been asserted
Printed in China

The authorized representative in the EEA is
Penguin Random House Ireland, Morrison Chambers,
32 Nassau Street, Dublin D02 YH68

A CIP catalogue record for this book is available from the British Library
ISBN: 978–0–241–48881–2
All correspondence to:
Puffin Books, Penguin Random House Children's
One Embassy Gardens, 8 Viaduct Gardens, London SW11 7BW